*Printing from
a Stone*
The Story of Lithography

S. CARL HIRSCH

Printing from a Stone

The Story of Lithography

THE VIKING PRESS / *New York*

Copyright © 1967 by S. Carl Hirsch
All rights reserved
First published in 1967 by The Viking Press, Inc.
625 Madison Avenue, New York, N. Y. 10022
Published simultaneously in Canada by
The Macmillan Company of Canada Limited
Library of Congress catalog card number: 67-13605
763   1. History of lithography
655.3   1. Printing

Printed in U. S. A.

For the Barnes family

Acknowledgments

I would like to express my appreciation to the following for their efforts to improve the manuscript, to offer helpful suggestions, and to provide valuable research materials: Dr. Clinton Adams, Dean of the College of Fine Arts, University of New Mexico; Michael H. Bruno and Robert Reed, Graphic Arts Technical Foundation; Dr. Paul J. Hartsuch, Editor, *The Graphic Arts Monthly;* Bertha von Moschzisker, Director, The Print Club, Philadelphia; William A. Schroeder, Educational Director, Lithographers and Photoengravers International Union; June Wayne, Director, Tamarind Lithography Workshop; Dr. R. Arnim Winkler, Munich, Germany; and the staff of the Stadtarchiv, Munich, Germany. I am also grateful to Robert Halloch, of Local One of the Amalgamated Lithographers of America, for his help in obtaining illustrations for the book.

Contents

List of Illustrations

Printing from
a Stone
The Story of Lithography

1

Chapter and Verse

This is a story of stones—not the stones from which mankind first fashioned tools, nor the stones with which men built the great centers of civilization, nor the stones which they carved to express their loftiest ideals.

In ancient times, inscriptions chiseled on stone helped to convey knowledge. But for all the arduous labors of the stone-carver, he produced only a single image. In contrast, the stones of this story served to duplicate words and pictures again and again, in many identical copies.

These stones were the foundation of a kind of printing called lithography. The method is described in the very word *lithography,* which comes from two Greek words: *lithos,* meaning stone, and *graphos,* writing.

Printing by lithography began in 1798, when it was discovered how words written with a crayon on a block of limestone could be repeatedly reproduced. Like other forms of printing, lithography is a method of making many copies of an image from an inked surface. It is in the great tradition of the printed picture and the printed word.

For hundreds of years, printing has been a lantern of learning that is passed from one generation to the next. A store of learning is contained in the pages of an encyclopedia. A scientific journal is published in Geneva and read eagerly in Jakarta. The printed wisdom of Gandhi has helped to solve problems in Gadsden, Alabama. For almost two hundred years, the printed words in America's Declaration of Independence have been a beacon for the world.

The history of printing is closely linked with man's search for knowledge and his struggles for freedom. Lithography is part of this history and this heritage. If the chronicle of printing can be thought of as a book, lithography would be a comparatively late chapter, but one filled with fascinating verses. A brilliant invention, it was based on an entirely new principle of printing, used novel materials, and developed in unexpected ways. And most interesting of all were the people who helped to make lithography the important factor that it is in today's world.

What is a lithograph? It may be an artist's original print—a masterpiece hanging in a museum—or a reproduction of that lithograph printed in a magazine. It may be a birthday card or a label on a soup can. This book is an example of lithography.

Lithography is produced today in a wide variety of ways and serves many needs, from the huge quantities of printed matter required in the modern business world to rare works of art which enrich men's lives.

A busy but pleasant workshop in Los Angeles is devoted to the art of the lithograph. A group of creative people are making drawings directly on stone. The magic of color is achieved by matching images on several stones. Prints are pulled on sheets of fine handmade paper. The usual edition of the finished lithograph at this studio is twenty copies, no more. The methods are the same as those used a century ago.

In contrast, there is modern commercial lithography. A typical plant may be found in Chicago, its huge presses thundering through the night. One press is fed by two giant rolls of paper, each weighing more than a ton. As the wide paper ribbon webs its way at high speed through the maze of flashing rollers, past the many color units, in and out of the automatic dryer, cutter, and folder, a book is being produced.

From the far end of the press flows an endless stream of thirty-two-page color-printed sheaves. These forms will be folded into signatures—each a segment of a book soon to appear in school classrooms, a new textbook in world history.

The making of books has its own history. To trace the story to its source, one must go back in time a thousand years, move thousands of miles in space to the evergreen uplands of central China. The speed of the modern world slows to the pace of the old Orient. The roar of machinery fades to the hum of scholars at a Chinese temple.

2

Steps to Stone

In the mist of an ancient morning, students make their way up the steep and stony path to their classes. On the silent mountain, one hears only the soft chanting of hymns and a bell from the village far below. In the tradition of old China, the silk-clad students walk in file, a few paces behind their teachers.

Inside the broad-eaved temple, the scribes are already at work. Seated on mats in a circle, they slowly copy the words from a large scroll. These are the writings of Confucius, almost destroyed in the course of a series of wars and disasters. They are being copied by hand.

At the door of the temple stand many stone slabs. On each of them some of the words of Confucius have been carved. The tablets were ordered engraved by the emperor to make doubly sure that the ancient teaching would be preserved.

One thought must have occurred to many of these students as they passed the tablets each day. If only the carved stones could somehow be used to print the scriptures, it would mean that there would be enough copies for everyone.

The slabs, however, presented a stumbling block. Some kind of lampblack ink might be applied to the stone, and then a piece of paper made from the bark of mulberry trees could be pressed against the surface. Undoubtedly this method would produce a printed black page, with the white characters clearly visible. But something else was also clear. Each one of the printed characters would be in reverse.

As no one had a solution to this problem, the riddle remained, and years passed without an answer.

At last, there came one who knew. While the students watched, he moistened a piece of paper and laid it on the flat stone. With a stiff brush he pressed the thin paper down into each of the tiny grooves made by the engraved words.

After dipping a silk pad in ink, he rubbed it lightly over the entire paper. When he pulled the blackened paper from the stone, it bore the words of the text, untouched by the ink. As if by magic, the ancient writing appeared in white against the black background, distinct and readable.

The paper was now a page—the page of a book. It was the kind of page that could be produced again and again in the same manner, from the same stone.

The actual origin of stone-rubbing is lost in the haze of time. But from what is known of that period in Chinese history, this type of book printing probably arose in some such fashion more than a thousand years ago.

A stone-rubbing made from a monument cast in 1107 A.D., and inscribed with an image of Confucius and his disciple. (Field Museum of Natural History.)

The Chinese also experimented with printing directly from page-size wooden blocks on which the writing had been carved in reverse. Artisans then realized the advantage of having each word on its own small individual block, so that the separate wooden pieces could be used again whenever the words appeared in the text. So the wood blocks were cut into pieces.

Soon methods were found for making these pieces of movable type more durable. Each character was carved in relief on a small block of wet clay and hardened in a kiln. Such pieces of porcelain type could be used repeatedly and arranged in any sequence for producing a printed page.

Long before it appeared in the Western world, printing in such forms was known in China. The Chinese, however, had not mastered the basic technique of lithography. Chinese stone-rubbing was a way of printing from stone but it was totally different in principle from the lithography which was to appear in Europe centuries later.

The technique of stone-rubbing has come down to us as coin-rubbing, a rainy-day pastime of children the world over. It is done by placing a piece of paper over a coin, then rubbing the paper gently with a soft pencil.

As for the Oriental methods of producing printed books, they remained Chinese secrets for hundreds of years—but only because

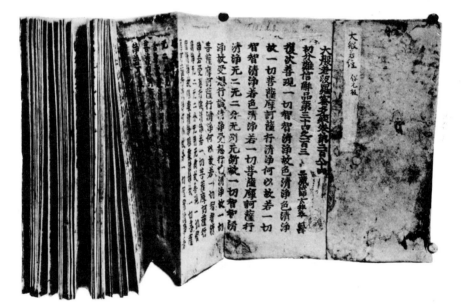

Part of the Buddhist scriptures, translated from Sanskrit into Chinese, was printed in this folded-book form in 1157 A.D.

of the lack of communication and interchange between East and West.

The trade routes between Asia and Europe before the fifteenth century were long and difficult. It was a five-year journey by the so-called Silk Route—overland across the vast reaches of China, through the high mountain passes of Tibet, by camel caravan across the Gobi Desert to Samarkand and Bukhara, then by the Black Sea or the Caspian Sea to the ports of Europe. Since traders traveled only short portions of the journey, goods changed from hand to hand and ideas had to be relayed from language to language.

The Chinese art of papermaking did travel that route. Gradually, paper appeared farther and farther to the West; it was finally brought to Europe by the Arabs.

Prior to the fifteenth century the Western world had written on materials such as papyrus, made from the matted fiber of a marsh reed. Other writing surfaces, such as parchment or vellum, were made from animal skins. These materials were either too

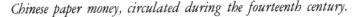

Chinese paper money, circulated during the fourteenth century.

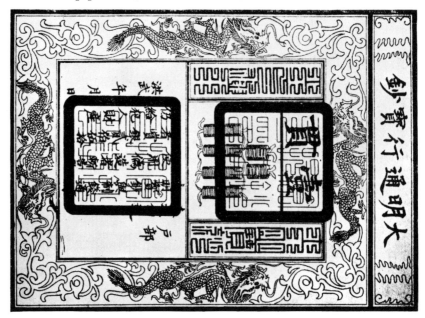

fragile or too costly. Gradually, they gave way to the Oriental invention, paper made by drying out a watery pulp of vegetable fibers.

European travelers in the Orient brought back samples of something that the West had never seen—paper money. In fact, Europeans were astonished to learn that in China valuable goods and hours of labor were exchanged for a piece of printed paper.

Some of the Chinese inventions were brought to Europe by the well-traveled Polo family, gem merchants of Venice. The youngest member, Marco, wandered about China in the thirteenth century and undoubtedly saw printing being done. However, there is no direct evidence that the Chinese techniques ever reached Europe.

Johann Gutenberg was born in the German city of Mainz in about 1397. The exact date of his birth, and many of the other facts about him, were not recorded. But it is known that Gutenberg was skilled in cutting gems and polishing mirrors, and that he set out to discover a practical method for printing books.

Court records show that Gutenberg was deep in debt, that he lost everything he had—his shop, his tools, his business—to moneylenders. Contemporary files of the French royalty reveal that the king of France once sent a secret agent to Mainz to learn about Gutenberg's invention.

Like other inventors, Gutenberg based his work on the discoveries of those who had gone before. Printing would have been quite impractical without paper—which was not being manufactured in Europe until Gutenberg's century. For the invention of paper, Gutenberg was indebted to a Chinese named Ts'ai Lun, who made the first paper from vegetable substances in the year 105 A.D.

The idea of the screw-type printing press he borrowed from the wine maker. He had only to change the bed of the press so that it would hold a page of type instead of a cluster of grapes.

Gutenberg owed his knowledge of casting metal to the silver-smiths of his time. And for the designs of his type, he was in-debted to the scribes—who were eventually left unemployed be-cause of Gutenberg's invention. The inventor copied the form of the letters that were used in handwritten manuscripts. To this day, many styles of type are based on the light and heavy strokes of the scribe's pen.

Whereas the inks used for printing in China had been water-soluble, Gutenberg used ink that contained oil to make it stick to the surface of the metal type.

As for movable type, the Chinese had this idea centuries before Gutenberg. However, it was probably not fully developed in China because the Chinese language is not alphabetical. It is made up of thousands of characters, each a separate word, and hence would have required an enormous quantity of individual pieces of type. Gutenberg's printed language was Latin. Including the full capi-tal and lower-case alphabets, numerals, and punctuation, Guten-berg's stock of type consisted of less than a hundred different characters.

Once he had gathered together the knowledge available to him, Gutenberg was confronted with the greatest problem of all—how to form type that was readable, durable, and suitable for assem-bling and printing.

Gutenberg finally produced type by a threefold process. He learned to fashion a hard-metal punch tipped with a sculptured letter of the alphabet. The punch was then hammered into a block of soft metal so as to form a mold. Into this mold, hot metal was poured. When it cooled and hardened, this bit of metal was a stick of type—the very core of Gutenberg's discovery.

Thus, by the middle of the fifteenth century, Europeans knew how to mold movable type out of metal. Paper was available. Most important of all, the mood of Europe was restless and eager

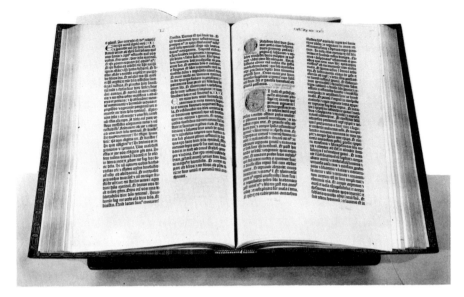

First printed Bible, known as the Gutenberg, printed in 1455 in Latin and bound in two volumes. (New York Public Library.)

for learning. In short, the Western world was ready to go to press.

Gutenberg's first printed books were Latin grammar textbooks. In his time Latin was an important key to learning. It was the international language of all recorded knowledge, including science.

Within a short span of years, the bulk of mankind's accumulated wisdom was set down in printed books.

As explorers discovered new worlds beyond the seas, so did great numbers of people discover the world of books which was previously beyond their reach.

In the year that Columbus set sail for the New World, a group of Bavarian printers recorded a wealth of learning in a thick encyclopedia called *The Nuremberg Chronicle.* Its low price made it available to large numbers of people who had never before owned a book.

Printed maps appeared for the first time. New books on natural science and medicine were enhanced by pictures. Some books, such as those illustrated with engravings by the German artist Albrecht Dürer, were works of art.

The Polish astronomer Copernicus came down from his roof top to write a book which revealed that the earth moved around the sun.

Never before had so much knowledge been available to ordinary men. Printing was a miracle that brought books out of closed and cloistered places and into the hands of millions. And with books readily available, men in growing numbers learned to read.

This was a revolution in black and white. In turn, there followed a series of upheavals in forms of government and in religious thought, in travel and trade, in science and art.

From the very outset of printing, people had to defend the right to publish and to read. The spread of books and learning did not receive the same joyful welcome everywhere. There were those in power who feared the demands that educated citizens would make.

In America the British governor of Virginia, Sir William Berkeley, vowed in 1671 that ignorance—and colonial rule—would prevail. "I thank God we have not free schools or printing; and I hope we shall not have, these hundred years," Sir William wrote to his monarch. "For learning has brought disobedience and heresy and sects in the world; and printing has divulged them and libels against the government. God keep us from both."

Such voices of darkness were silenced, however, as men began to lay claim to a wide range of freedoms as their birthright—and among these was freedom of the press.

In those years, handmade type was slowly and laboriously set in page form. The presses were clumsy wooden screw-type, hand-operated affairs. And yet, books began to appear at a lively rate.

In the centuries that followed there were few basic changes

in the methods used to print the first books. The favorite technique of printers then, as now, is called letterpress. In this process the type or the printing plate is formed so that the actual printing surface stands out in high relief. Words are printed from pieces of type, each letter of the alphabet appearing in reverse on its own little pedestal. Pictures are similarly printed from plates prepared in such a way that the printing image is raised above the base. Once inked, this raised surface comes into contact with the paper, thus printing the image.

Another variety of printing, called gravure, also has a long history of development. Gravure produces the kind of print known as an engraving. The engraver does not use a raised line from which to print. Instead he cuts the image into the plate with a sharp tool called a graver. He then inks the plate and carefully wipes the surface clean and dry, allowing the ink to remain only in the grooves. When great pressure is applied, the thirsty fibers of the paper soak up some of the ink, thus producing the engraved image.

A different form of gravure is called etching. A metal plate, usually copper, is coated with a thin layer of wax. The etcher carves his image into the wax coating, cutting just deep enough to reach the surface of the metal. The next step is to pour acid on the surface. Where the wax coating remains the metal plate is left intact. But wherever grooves are cut through the wax, the acid eats, or etches, its way into the metal. In the final stages of making an etching, the coating is removed. The plate is inked and then its surface is wiped dry. The image can now be transferred to paper in the press.

Both letterpress and gravure processes are "two-level" methods of printing. To the eye, both kinds of plates have a sculptured appearance. Both are rough to the touch. Both depend on a difference in height between the image and the nonimage areas of the printing plate.

Seen in cross section, the letterpress plate appears quite similar to a gravure plate. In letterpress, the ink is on the peaks and plateaus. In **gravure**, the ink is in the lowlands and valleys.

LETTERPRESS   GRAVURE   LITHOGRAPHY

It was not until the end of the eighteenth century that a completely different method of printing came into being—lithography. This was not relief printing. It used neither a raised nor a depressed printing surface. Instead, it achieved the "impossible"—printing from a flat plane!

3

Oil and Water

The process by which this page was printed owes its origin to an ingenious man named Aloys Senefelder whose life was filled with hardship.

He came from a background which hardly prepared him for the discovery he was to make. His invention was achieved through persistent and painstaking effort over a long period of time.

Although he fought to keep his invention from being stolen from him, he was turned out of his own shop by shrewd and unscrupulous men. And in the end, he profited very little from his ingenuity—except in terms of the gratitude of the generations which were to come.

Senefelder's life strangely parallels that of his predecessor, Gutenberg. The two men were separated in time by more than three
hundred years and in distance by less than three hundred miles.
It seems that both Gutenberg and Senefelder were impelled on-
ward by a glittering goal, the vision of the printed page. Both
belonged to periods of history when bold new ideas were being
advanced, ideas that needed to be examined by ever-widening
circles of readers.

The printing arts flourished in the very center of Europe. If
Gutenberg's town of Mainz was the cradle of printing, then
Senefelder's Bavarian city of Munich must be marked as the place
where lithography was born.

Bavaria was a land of great monasteries where monks had
worked for centuries slowly copying the old manuscripts. The
ancient abbey of Oberzell was one in which the cowled brothers
sat in cubicles scribing their books with the quill pen, letter by
letter, page by page. They could not have known that their monas-
tery would someday house a printing-press factory.

Though born in Prague, Aloys Senefelder had lived in the
Bavarian city of Munich since he was six years old. In 1792, at
the age of twenty-one, he had suddenly become the sole sup-
porter of a large family. His father, who was an actor, had died,
leaving Frau Senefelder with nine children, of whom Aloys was
the eldest. The family was already in debt, and the outlook was
not good.

Young Senefelder had achieved some success as a playwright
with an amateur theater group. However, it was no easy matter
for an unknown playwright to find a publisher. As for having
his plays printed, he could not possibly afford the printer's bill.

Aloys walked the rain-wet streets of the old city with its
steeply gabled roofs, its bell towers and clock towers set against
the dark green forests and the distant Alps. The gentle spring
rain had laid a glistening film over the stone streets. Here and

there were dry patches, where a layer of oil or grease on the limestone paving shed the water. The perplexed young man was deep in thought as he crossed the square toward the stone-paved riverbank where the Isar gathered the cold green waters from the nearby mountain streams.

The only solution for Aloys was to become his own publisher and printer. But how? This was the question that occupied him as he walked the wet cobbled streets of Munich.

How could he have known that the answer would be found in the stones beneath his feet?

When Aloys Senefelder set about becoming a printer, he literally had to "start from scratch."

His early experiments were in copper engraving. The first problem he faced was an old one: Whatever words he scribed on the metal plate appeared in print on paper backward. This might have been enough to stop many people—but not Senefelder. He plunged into the arduous task of teaching himself to write in reverse.

He spent long hours writing backward. Then he practiced with the graver, carving the words into the copper so that they read from right to left instead of left to right.

If not too difficult, this method soon proved to be too expensive for the penniless youth. The copper could be ground smooth and re-used, but with much grinding and polishing, the costly plate soon became paper-thin.

It was then that Aloys secured from a stonemason a thick slab of Bavarian limestone. The stone was soft enough to be grooved with the tool and yet hard enough for his practice engraving.

The resourceful young fellow made his own inks. He dabbled in mixing chemicals to etch his plates. He invented a kind of waxy crayon which he could use to cover up mistakes when the graver slipped.

And so the days passed for Aloys in tireless trial and error, in patient practice and experimentation. He was spurred forward in his work by home problems which seemed to mount each day.

Around Aloys Senefelder swirled the busy life of Munich, a city of printers and ironmakers, brewers and goldsmiths. The industrious people of the Bavarian capital were skilled craftsmen, but they also knew how to enjoy their leisure time. They promenaded in the grassy parks, danced in the beer gardens, filled the cafés at the close of the bustling market days, knew a hundred ways to make a tasty sausage, and packed the many fine theaters for which the city was famous.

Aloys now had little time for the theater. His driving desire to become a play publisher left him no opportunity for playwriting.

However, he was soon to enact a scene which was to set the stage for the larger drama of his life. It began one morning with the sound of the brass knocker on the Senefelder door. The laundress had come for the soiled linens.

Immediately a frantic search began. The laundry was ready. But where was a piece of paper on which to record the list of towels, sheets, pillowcases, and whatnot?

The children darted through the house, hunting for paper. Mrs. Senefelder called out to Aloys. There was a sharpness in her tone. After all, it was Aloys, forever experimenting with his printing, who had used up every scrap of blank paper in the house.

In despair, Aloys turned to what was handy—a homemade crayon, a clean slab of stone. He soon had the list jotted down and the laundress was on her way.

It was some time later that Aloys again took notice of the stone and the words scribbled on it with the greasy crayon. On some bold notion, he treated the stone with a mild acid. The chemicals bubbled and ate into portions of the stone—but not that part of the stone protected by the crayon writing. More acid, and soon the words stood out in relief. As he described it later, the written portions were raised "about the thickness of a playing card."

Aloys applied water to the stone, and then a greasy homemade ink. The ink adhered only to the greasy writing. Eagerly he pressed a sheet of paper against the surface of the stone. The words were printed in reverse—but sharp and clear. So many sheets, towels, and pillowcases!

More water, more ink, more paper—and now another printed copy and still another.

Aloys Senefelder quickly realized that by this method he could print a page of writing or a sheet of music, or reproduce a drawing. He had found a new way of producing a printing plate.

Aloys was delighted with his discovery. And yet he knew that this was merely a method for putting a raised image on stone. At this point, he had found only another form of relief printing not basically different in principle from the letterpress methods long in use. But the stone which served as his printing plate would soon lead him to the invention of a totally new printing process.

Portrait of Senefelder, a lithograph drawn from life on stone by the artist Lorenz Quaglio in 1818. (New York Public Library.)

4

The Keystone

Some stories of great inventions seem to be greatly invented stories. Did the explosive idea of the steam engine really come to James Watt as he sat watching the tea kettle boil over? And was the lightning conductor invented because Benjamin Franklin accidentally chose a stormy day on which to go fly a kite? It seems that these homespun tales can hardly be the whole truth.

As for Aloys Senefelder and the laundry list, we have his own account of the actual incident. However, all his life Senefelder continued to explain: "I did not invent stone-printing through a lucky accident." The piece of good luck was merely a breakthrough which led him on and on through hundreds of additional experiments to his ultimate achievement.

Mere chance does sometimes play a role in great discoveries. But it is the ingenuity of the inventor that enables him to turn a fortunate accident into a finished achievement. In the case of Senefelder, ingenuity was supplemented by a lot of hard work under the most trying circumstances.

Senefelder now had a method for printing, but where would he find the money for paper and ink, for presses and stones? In despair, the youth thought of every possible source. At last, he had a plan.

In those days, Bavaria was in the path of war. Napoleon's armies were storming across continents. In every country of central Europe, the air was filled with the rumors of trouble and the sound of marching men.

It was the custom in Bavaria that the sons of the well-to-do could buy their way out of the six years of required military service by hiring a substitute. The price was two hundred gulden. Aloys dreamed of what he could do with such a sum of money.

Although the period of military service seemed hopelessly long, he told himself that once he had finished his basic training, he could come back to his workshop on furloughs. If things went well with his printing business, he thought, he could even pay others to do his sentry duty. "And the six years will soon pass . . ."

This was the daydream that brought the youth face to face with the officer in brass and braid who interviewed the new recruits.

"Your name?"

"Aloys Senefelder."

"When and where were you born?"

"I was born in 1771, in the city of Prague, Bohemia."

The officer dropped his pen. The interview was at an end. Didn't Senefelder know that under a new decree no foreigners were allowed in the Bavarian army?

Aloys pleaded that he had lived in Bavaria since he was six years old. But the law was clear. His military career was over. So were his chances of securing two hundred gulden.

But Senefelder had no time for despair. With the help of a friend, he soon had an order for printing which promised not only a trickle of gulden but further orders as well. The Countess von Herting was planning an affair to mark the death of the composer Mozart. Senefelder was given the job of printing a hundred and fifty copies of a cantata written for the occasion.

Aloys rejoiced. At last, things were going his way—or seemed to be. He was so encouraged that he decided to present his invention to the Bavarian Royal Academy of Sciences. He had heard that large sums of money were granted by the Royal Academy, sometimes for inventions that later proved to be worthless. Even more important, a favorable recommendation by the institution could bring one fame and a prosperous future.

Aloys' hopes were high as he waited in the anteroom of the Royal Academy. He was a sturdy youth, with a full jaw, wide-set eyes, and a deep-lined brow. His unruly hair was brushed back, his shirt open at the throat in the romantic manner of the times.

At last came Herr von Vachiery, the vice-president of the Academy. He told the young man that the council had been much impressed with the invention. Aloys felt a surge of jubilation.

The vice-president went on to question Senefelder closely about his expenses. A total of six gulden for the building of his press, wasn't that it? Aloys explained that his mother had paid a house carpenter that sum to construct the press.

The councilors of the Royal Academy would make a generous contribution, said Herr von Vachiery. Aloys listened eagerly. They had decided to award him twice the amount of his expenses— twelve gulden.

One of Senefelder's crude hand-operated presses. (Munich Museum.)

Aloys did not forget to voice his thanks. But he had difficulty hiding his disappointment. Twelve gulden. What a blow to his hopes!

The youth hurried home. A few gold pieces would help. But what he had sought more than the payment of money was the support of the Royal Academy in establishing the importance of his invention. He realized that he had come before the Academy as an unknown and penniless petitioner, without influential sponsors. But he had hoped that his achievement would speak for itself.

Senefelder began work on the printing order for the Countess. And because he wanted it to turn out perfectly, he designed and built a new press. But as the days moved swiftly toward the Mozart memorial, Aloys' troubles mounted. The first impressions of the music were poor. Something was wrong.

Senefelder spent days tinkering with the new press. Nothing

seemed to help. Somehow the proper pressure could not be brought to bear on the rollers. He added weights, but this only resulted in cracking the stone plate. He used a thicker slab of stone, and added more weights.

As Senefelder worked one day under his pulleys and levers, a rope suddenly gave way. A three-hundred-pound weight came crashing down. Luckily, he managed to turn away just in time. Senefelder had almost given his life to lithography!

It was a sad moment when Aloys finally had to inform the Countess that he would not be able to deliver her printing. Only later did he discover the reason for his trouble. The wooden roller on his old press, which had a crack in it, somehow gripped the stone and the paper exactly right. His new press had been made too well to work properly.

In the difficult days and years that followed, Aloys Senefelder threw himself into his experimental work with great vigor and spirit. He did not permit himself a moment of doubt.

At last came that series of steps which led straight to the key of lithography. It is interesting to trace these final stages, each one following the last almost as a matter of course. Here the mind of the inventor is revealed, and his line of reasoning. Fortunately, we have it all set down in diary fashion, in Senefelder's own words.

The year was 1798. Senefelder was at work reproducing by means of stone some drawings from old engraved copper plates. He made an engraved print from the plate in the usual fashion, using his greasy ink. While the ink was still wet, he pressed the paper against a clean stone.

The greasy image was transferred completely to the stone. But this time, Senefelder did not etch the stone with acid. He wondered if he could print from the flat stone as it was. He asked himself: "Could not the stone itself be prepared so that it would take ink only on the parts covered with the greasy image?"

Knowing that ink would not adhere to a wet surface, since oil and water do not mix, he applied first water to the stone and then the printing ink. The method produced a clear reproduction of the drawing on paper, without a smudge. "I found that in this way I could make as many impressions as I pleased," he later wrote. "Simply wetting the stone and applying ink produced the same result each time."

So began lithography—a printing process different from any that had come before. And yet, like so many great inventions, it was the result of adding one new idea to a great many old ones.

The inventor pieces together a thousand bits and fragments of knowledge—and then he adds a key piece of his own that makes the whole thing possible.

An inventor is like a stonemason building a great arch. The structure rises upward through a pattern of stresses and thrusts—until at last its stability must depend on a single stone. Aloys Senefelder provided such a stone, the keystone of lithography.

From the outset, the nineteenth century was marked by an unprecedented spread of the printed word. In many European cities, daily newspapers began to appear. Journals and pamphlets promoted every new cause. Great libraries were thrown open to the public. Ordinary men read history—and made it.

In the United States, Thomas Jefferson championed his exciting idea of "Hundred Schools"—a system of free, universal, public education, with one school for every hundred children. "Enlighten the people generally," Jefferson said, "and tyranny and oppression of body and mind will vanish like evil spirits at the dawn of day."

It was at this time that Aloys Senefelder opened a new chapter in the history of printing.

His invention had to be carefully explained and exhibited. His idea was so daring that he could hardly get people to believe it worked without demonstrating the process.

The materials Senefelder used were original and strange. His ingredients came not from the chemist but from the kitchen. Among the items that he used in making his crayons and inks were sugar and laundry soap, goose grease and lampblack, beef suet and beeswax.

Like his tools, his first presses were homemade, each with two wooden rollers which he cranked by sheer muscle power.

As for the limestone, its origin was along the banks of the Danube, not more than fifty miles from Senefelder's home. This particular grade of stone was well known. It had been used for centuries for paving-blocks. The famous piazza at St. Peter's in Rome is lined with it.

Yellow or gray in appearance, the Bavarian stone is porous. Grease penetrates the stone surface so that an impression made on its surface with a greasy crayon or ink becomes fixed in the stone. The area of the stone not covered by grease is able to hold a film of water. As long as it is wet, this part of the surface rejects the oil-based printing ink.

These were the things that Aloys explained again and again during the early years of the new century. He traveled from one end of Europe to the other, demonstrating how one could actually print from a flat surface.

With a crayon, he made some simple drawing on a smooth stone. For example, he would sketch roughly the map of Europe, filling in the land area with greasy crayon. The surrounding seas he left blank.

Then he wet the surface of the stone. But the water remained only in the blank areas representing the seas. The grease-covered image of Europe shed the water completely. Next, he inked the stone. The ink adhered to the land area of Europe which he had drawn with the greasy crayon. Not a bit of the greasy ink remained in the wet sea portion of the stone.

The paper pressed against the stone came away with a clean

impression of the continent, the land area solid black on the white paper.

"This method does not depend on either the raising or lowering of the design," Senefelder explained. "It depends on the fact that the design is coated with a substance which has a chemical affinity to the ink. Furthermore, because all parts of the plate that are to remain blank have been covered with water, they repel the ink." An oil-based ink adheres naturally to a greasy image, and it does not mix readily with water.

Senefelder had discovered how the well-known chemical properties of grease and water could be put to the service of mankind. But in explaining the chemistry of the lithographic process, he clearly acknowledged his debt to Johann Gutenberg. For Gutenberg had developed the greasy ink which made printing from metal possible. And it was this same type of greasy ink which enabled Senefelder to print from stone.

Senefelder's invention did not have the same impact as did the newly invented steam engine, which was already turning the mills of Munich. Nor did Senefelder create as much excitement as did the young German inventor who rode through town one day on a contraption which later became known as the bicycle.

But slowly, gradually, lithography did begin to make its imprint on the times.

In the year 1808, Senefelder published a reproduction of an old prayer book illustrated by Albrecht Dürer. This book, faithfully copied on stone by a contemporary artist, revealed in a striking way the possibilities of lithography as an art medium. The quality of the printing was so fine that the new process was soon being discussed throughout Europe. Wherever lithography was demonstrated, there was amazement over the speed and the fidelity with which an image could be duplicated.

A "mechanized" press on which Senefelder widely demonstrated his new lithographic process. (Munich Museum.)

From its beginnings, it was clear that lithography would develop in two directions. Well-known artists quickly adopted it as a medium for their art. At the same time, lithography began to be used by commercial printers as a fast and inexpensive method.

Senefelder continued his creative efforts to improve his "stone-printing," as he called it. To overcome the difficulty of drawing the image in reverse on the stone, Senefelder developed what he called "the transfer method."

By this means, the artist could draw his crayon picture on a sheet of special coated paper. When the paper was pressed against a lithographic stone, the greasy image was transferred to the stone, becoming reversed from right to left in the process. Once the stone was inked, the image could be imprinted on paper, again being reversed from right to left, so that the final picture would appear just as the artist had drawn it. While some artists adopted the transfer method, others preferred to work directly on stone.

The transfer method was later used widely in commercial printing, for text as well as for pictures. The first operation in printing text by the transfer method was to set the type in the same way as for letterpress printing. Then a proof made with greasy ink could be transferred to the stone to obtain a clear impression of the text in the lithographic press.

In Munich in the early years of the nineteenth century, Aloys Senefelder was aware of the new machinery being used and knew that the days of the hand-driven printing press were numbered. He developed an idea for a water-driven press. The far-sighted Senefelder described its operation, "wherein the damping and inking of the stones should be done not by hands but by the mechanism of the press itself, which, in addition, could be operated by water and thus work almost without human intervention."

Unfortunately for Aloys Senefelder, he had no head for business. While others might have made a fortune from his invention, Aloys was dogged by countless problems and cruel poverty. He was repeatedly tricked and betrayed in dealings with friends and even close relatives. He was overly trusting when he should have been cautious. In the commercial world there were many who took advantage of his honesty and generosity.

Senefelder was proud of his invention. And he took delight in explaining it to almost anyone who would listen. "I have been criticized for my frankness," he declared. "Many have said I could have been a millionaire if I had kept my art a secret. But I could not have succeeded in this way. I could never resist making public anything that I discovered to benefit mankind."

Far from keeping lithography a secret, he revealed everything he knew about the process. In 1818, he wrote a book called *A Complete Course of Lithography*, explaining how he came to invent it, and how this method could be used for almost every kind of printing. It is still one of the best books on the fundamental principles of the process.

Senefelder patiently trained workmen in the techniques of lithography. Many of them went on to establish successful business enterprises. In later life, the impoverished Senefelder remarked sadly that he would consider himself lucky if he could obtain work under one of his former apprentices.

Although he never became rich, Senefelder did finally win recognition. Even the Royal Academy, which had once granted him only a few gulden, gave him a gold medal and its full approval. Most important to Senefelder, however, was that in his declining years he could see that his process was at last being widely used.

Lithography seemed to find its greatest usefulness in those countries where the newest ideas of the age needed an outlet: in the United States, where democracy was a bright new reality seeking further expression; in France, where restless men were writing the new watchwords of freedom.

5

Signed: H. D.

For Honoré Daumier, lithography was a stepping stone to greatness. He drew on stone an unforgettable record of his time.

Daumier's parents had been small-town folks. At least, that was
how these new arrivals from Marseilles were regarded by their
Paris neighbors.

"And the boy—what does he want to do?" asked the landlady
of the rooming house where the family lived.

"My Honoré?" Madame Daumier shrugged and turned to her
young son. "You don't know, do you? Or perhaps you don't
want to do anything."

"Oh, yes," the young fellow cried out, "I want to draw!"

Honoré's father was a mender of broken windows. He shouted

his trade in the city streets, his voice mingling with the cries of the vendors, the music of the hurdy-gurdy, the clatter of horse-drawn wagons.

In his own way the elder Daumier was a poet. He had an ear for the music of words—and his son proved to have an eye for the rhythm of lines.

The son of a poor glazier could not afford art lessons. But Honoré had little interest in copying the old masterpieces in the museums or sketching arrangements of flowers and fruits in the art schools of Montmartre. Instead he studied art from life—the life of the city. He was happy working as a lawyer's messenger, seeing Paris as a series of finely drawn pictures, an endlessly fascinating pattern of forms vibrant with human drama.

On his way through the law courts, he paused to watch a poor family being dragged off to debtors' prison. In the streets, he marched along with a demonstration of striking weavers, their red banners flying. He daily encountered many crippled beggars, the veterans of Napoleon's wars in Europe and Africa. His errands took him past the ornate palace of the Tuileries, where the self-made emperor had held court.

The French Revolution, more than forty years earlier, had failed to achieve for the people of France the democratic liberties for which they yearned. Paris, the hearth of the Revolution, still smoldered. In its ancient streets, embattled shopkeepers, laborers, students, and artisans continued the fight for freedom.

The cobblestone was a symbol of Paris and the traditional weapon of its people. Pitched battles were fought in the streets. The people tore up the street pavings, using the cobbles to build barricades and to unloose deadly showers of stones.

It was a different kind of stone that Daumier used when he joined in the struggle for political freedom. He learned about lithography, the recently invented method of printing from stone that had been used with great success by some of the outstanding artists of France. He tried it and found that it suited his needs. He was to become the first great artist whose life's work was centered in lithography.

Working for a small Paris newspaper, Daumier could earn a modest livelihood drawing lithographs. The newspaper encouraged Daumier to express his growing concern about social problems. In those years, brief struggles for liberty came as lightning flashes in an era heavily clouded with militarism and monarchy. And Daumier found himself caught up in the tempest of the times.

The newspaper was called *La Caricature*, a word that had come to mean a satirical drawing. Daumier's caricatures were clever character studies. He used slight exaggerations for the sake of truth, making humorous cartoon-like drawings that dealt with the topics of the day.

Daumier's chief target was Louis Philippe, the pear-shaped king of France who had betrayed his promises and who answered the demands for social reform by putting people in prison.

The publishers of *La Caricature* liked Daumier's lithographs. "See how cleverly he works on the stone," said one editor.

"Yes," came the reply, "he uses it to sharpen his wits!"

Honoré Daumier became more and more skilled at both caricature and lithography. He worked speedily under the discipline of a newspaper deadline. In fact, this seemed to improve his artistry. He developed a sureness of line. He learned to use the lithographic crayon with great effect, drawing a warm response from the cold stone.

Daumier worked from memory, and the people of Paris were his models. They were also his teachers, for he learned by sensing the public's response to his drawings. There were times when he knew that he had hit the mark, expressing the deepest feelings of the people on some burning issue.

The more successful his drawings, the more he drew the anger of the monarch. One rainy August night, on his way home from a nearby café, Daumier found the agents of the Crown waiting for him with a warrant for his arrest. King Louis Philippe had taken another victim—freedom of the press.

In Ste. Pélagie prison, which was filled with political victims, Daumier continued to develop his drawing skill and his hatred of injustice deepened. When he was released six months later, he lost no time in returning to the crayon and the stone.

There were days in the year 1834 when Daumier sat quietly in the gallery of the Chamber of Deputies. He observed searchingly as the talk droned on, as if he were trying to engrave on his mind each face, each gesture, each expression.

Daumier was not impressed by the high-sounding speeches. He knew this chamber as a hollow show of popular government. These deputies were supposed to represent the people of France. But, in fact, many of them were tearing away the last shreds of freedom. They passed harsh taxes on the people. They planned profitable new wars and colonial ventures. They fattened their own fortunes at the public expense.

On his way home one afternoon, Daumier entered the web of crooked streets that edged the river. He was a stocky, handsome young man, with dark eyes and a shock of thick wheat-colored hair.

The cut of his cape and his broad-brimmed hat identified him as an artist. And yet, he was not forever penciling a sketch book. He simply observed and recorded in his memory the street scenes that later would become lithographs. He looked and listened for the pulse of Parisian life.

He paused for a moment as a homebound worker was met in the street by his wife and child. The proud father could hardly restrain his joy at the sight of the infant. Daumier heard the

"Interior of an Omnibus: Seated between a Drunk and a Butcher"
was Daumier's caption for this lithograph, published in 1841.

young wife scold: "Don't laugh so loud; you'll make him cry!"

The artist noted a housewife washing the family laundry on the bank of the Seine. He crossed the river on the footbridge. Below, a family was bathing in the shallow water. The terrified son had wrapped himself around his father's neck. "Yes, I do want to learn to swim," Daumier heard the boy cry out, "but not in the water—not in the water!"

Daumier chuckled to himself and hurried to his studio on the Quai d'Anjou. He climbed the stairs to the large, bare room. There were a few tables and chairs, a cast-iron stove, and heaps of lithographic prints and proofs. On a raised platform were a number of small sculptured heads—each depicting a member of the

Chamber of Deputies. The artist went to work finishing the figures at high speed, as if to catch the impressions while they were still fresh in his mind. Marvelously, the little heads took final form under his fingers.

The sculptured heads were Daumier's preparation for a lithograph. These figures were his sketches—in clay.

At length, he went to a large table where his lithographic stones lay—a half-dozen of them. Five had unfinished drawings, to which he would later add more detail.

On the sixth large, clean stone, he began his drawing of the Chamber of Deputies. The stone had been ground and smoothed, but not highly polished. He selected his crayons from a box of short pieces. They were an assortment of hard and soft crayons, pointed and blunt.

Daumier drew swiftly, with broad, sure strokes, the stone recording the slightest pressure of the crayon. The artist worked carefully, knowing how sensitive the stone was to any touch—to a fingerprint. It seemed as if one could hardly breathe on the stone without leaving an impression. More than once, Daumier had saved a drawing by repressing an ill-timed sneeze.

As he worked from the clay figures Daumier's drawing began to show that distinctive style which was his. The Parisian novelist Balzac said of Daumier, "Here is a fellow who has Michelangelo under his skin!" The comparison with the great Italian sculptor is an apt one, for there is a sculptural quality in Daumier's drawings. True, he did not always work from clay models. But he did visualize his figures in the round, and they seem to stand in relief from the paper on which they were printed.

The background he sketched in quickly, trying to remember always that the final lithograph on paper would print in reverse from the way it appeared on the stone. As a boy he had been told to mind his "*p*'s and *q*'s." Later in life, he learned that this

Daumier's "The Legislative Belly" was drawn in 1834. (Metropolitan Museum of Art.)

phrase had its origin in the printing trade. The printer, working backward with his type, is apt to make mistakes with certain letters. Daumier's problem was with the letter N. On many of his speedily done lithographic prints, the N's appear backward.

Daumier lit his pipe and studied the stone. Slowly the drawing was taking shape. This was his impression of the corrupt and foolish members of the French parliament—his comment on the selfishness and greed of the legislators who fattened on the misery of the people. He decided to call the drawing "The Legislative Belly."

A few days later, the finished lithograph appeared in a shop window. A passerby stopped, amused. Another looked—and suddenly shrieked with raucous laughter. A crowd gathered and roared with glee.

Some were picking out the familiar figures. Yes, there they were, "all the king's men!" There was the goblin-like minister of finance who had grown fat in office. And the king's sly minister, looking like a rogue caught red-handed. And the banker-senator with the hawklike expression. And the tax collector, slumbering contentedly in his seat. What a joke!

Daumier had become a master at mockery. He used humor to pinprick the pompous deputies. Every line that he drew on stone was comic. With a few deft strokes of the crayon, he exposed the self-important statesmen to ridicule.

At one franc each, the lithographs sold by the thousands. They passed from hand to hand. Soon all Paris rocked with laughter.

Paris became very familiar with the signature "H. D." in the corner of a lithograph. From Daumier the citizens of this seething city could expect almost daily some pointed comment on the social problems of the times, or a humorous little sketch of Paris life, or a raging outcry against tyranny.

There were times when he argued in the newspaper office about the long-winded explanations that were often printed with his drawings. Daumier believed that each lithograph must stand on its own merits. "If my drawing says nothing to you," he told his editor, "it is bad. The printed words will not make it better."

Daumier saved his anger for those who stood in the way of human hopes. He was a warmhearted man with a deep love for the people.

He found his models in the cramped back streets and in the broad avenues of Paris, engaged in their work—the lamplighter and the street singer, the chimney sweep and the blacksmith. In these lithographs, Daumier seemed to draw life from the stone. He recorded the varied expressions of passengers being jostled together in a crowded horse-drawn omnibus. His portraits of a sad-eyed clown, of a family in the park, or of men in prison reflect the moods of the time, as well as his own feeling for humanity.

The artist was a tireless fighter against the small and large abuses that beset the common people of Paris. He put the scoundrels of his age on public display. Poking mild fun at lawyers, he did a series of lithographs showing them in the whole range of their pompous professional poses. He drew a grouchy land-lady, surrounded by numerous animal pets, telling a worried mother: "I do not rent to people with children!"

In Daumier's late years, Europe was once again being rushed headlong into armed conflict. With all his mastery of the lithog-rapher's art, Daumier unloosed his fury and his grief against the waste of war. It was said that in these bitter drawings "his crayon was dipped in acid."

In all, Daumier drew some four thousand lithographs. They appeared about twice a week over a period of forty years.

Although his drawings on stone were made for newspaper use, their value was not simply for a day. Many of them proved to be masterworks that today have still not lost their freshness or their greatness as art.

Daumier used lithography to make a powerful comment on the drama of his day, and also helped to establish it in mid-eighteenth century France as an important medium of fine art.

Meanwhile, in the United States, Senefelder's invention had been adopted to serve a somewhat different purpose.

6

"Eleven Hundred Subjects"

On a Monday night, January 13, 1840, the newsroom of the New York *Sun* was strangely empty. Every available reporter had been sent to the water front. The steamboat *Lexington,* with one hundred and thirty-five people aboard, was burning like a torch in Long Island Sound.

Newspapers were then staging a fierce competition in covering the news for "scoops." Along New York's newspaper row, every possible trick was turned to get the jump on the opposition papers. And the *Sun,* under the vigorous command of Moses Y. Beach, was seldom caught slumbering.

At a time shortly before the invention of the telegraph, Beach hired the swiftest couriers, the fastest horses, and the fleetest ships to carry the news. The *Sun* had even astounded New Yorkers when the paper began receiving news dispatches by carrier pigeon.

On this tragic January night, the *Sun* editor paced the deserted office. The burning of the *Lexington* was a big story, and he wanted the kind of coverage no other newspaper would have. He wanted more than mere words to describe the horror out in the Sound.

At length, he sent a messenger out into the blustery night. The boy found a small shop in Nassau Street bearing the sign: *N. Currier, Lithographer and Publisher.*

The message was brief. How soon could Currier produce a picture of the burning *Lexington?* The reply was swift. "Give me seventy-two hours!"

By Thursday of that week, the newsboys were out in the streets shouting "Extra—extra *Sun!*"

Across the page was Currier's large hand-drawn lithograph of

"Awful Conflagration of the Steam Boat Lexington *in Long Island Sound on Monday Evening." (Museum of the City of New York.)*

the *Lexington* tragedy. Flames, filling the sky, were whipped by a wild gale. Passengers were shown crowding the rail of the doomed ship, caught between the raging fire and the icy waters. Many of the lifeboats had turned over, dumping passengers into the sea. Scores of survivors could be seen in the water, clinging to bales of cotton from the ship's cargo, struggling for life. The artist had shown the full drama of the night in the newspaper picture.

It would be another fifty years before the era of practical newspaper photography. And today, at a time when instantaneous news pictures are available, Currier's feat might seem commonplace. In the 1840s, it was a sensation.

This was the period of the fast-growing "penny papers," when Americans were becoming more conscious of the outside world. In an America where illiteracy was still widespread, newspapers had suddenly become important. Where else could one learn of the opening of the door to Japan or of the stormy revolutions from one end of Europe to the other? Where else could one read of the new steamboats and steam trains, of the Battle of the Alamo and the adventures on the Oregon Trail?

A lithograph depicting such stories could make the reader feel as though he were an eyewitness at the scene. Currier's drawings on stone became popular. And he suddenly realized that he had a thriving business.

Currier's shop began to resemble a newspaper office. In lithographing news pictures, he literally left no stone unturned. Artist-reporters were dispatched to the sites of fires, shipwrecks, and flooded areas. In a perverse way, each new misfortune presented Currier with a fortunate new business opportunity.

Currier was not himself an artist, but he knew where he could hire the talent he needed. He was a shrewd businessman and he had a solid grounding in the technique of lithography.

Currier had learned the craft of stone-printing from a Boston family, the Pendletons. Shortly after Senefelder's book on lithography was published, John Pendleton had taken a trip to Europe, anxious to learn more about the new method of printing.

In 1825 he had brought back to the United States much technical information, a ton of lithographic stones, and two skilled French lithographers. When John Pendleton started his stone-printing business in Boston, he hired a fifteen-year-old apprentice, Nathaniel Currier.

The boy spent many hours laboriously grinding the stones. He watched the crayon artist Bischou at work on the drawings. He learned about the chemicals used to improve the printing quality of the greasy image on the stone. He mixed inks. He fed sheets into the press, working with the French press operator DuBois.

Young Currier was clever and learned quickly. In fact, he had mastered the process long before his five-year apprenticeship was finished. When he left Boston to strike out on his own, he was not even old enough to vote in the re-election of Andrew Jackson. But he was ready to begin his own business.

This blue-eyed young man with blond side whiskers had a pleasant personality. He listened carefully to the talk around him and responded to the changing ideas and tastes of a young and robust America.

Currier opened his lithography shop in New York City in 1834. It was the year that Aloys Senefelder died.

Two decades later, when Currier's firm was thriving, he hired James Merritt Ives, a short, swarthy young fellow, who became the bookkeeper. Ives proved to have some talent as an artist and many ideas about popular subjects that could be pictured in lithographs. This was the man Currier chose as a partner.

The partnership was to dominate lithography in America for a half-century. The firm name was to become a household word— Currier & Ives.

In thousands of lithographs, Currier & Ives presented a matchless portrait of America at mid-century. Today, these prints form a record of high historical value. They were even more exciting to the people who lived through those eventful years.

One January morning in 1848, a few bright pebbles were found in a California millstream. "Gold!" was the word tapped out over the newly invented telegraph circuits.

American families had been moving steadily into the plain states and the territory in the Southwest which had recently become part of the nation. But by the end of the year 1848, the migration roving westward had turned into a mad rush.

Nathaniel Currier lost no time in getting this story on stone. His artists worked at a feverish pace drawing pictures of the westward movement in all its colorful phases. In lithographs, he told the remarkable story of an America on the move, traveling by every available means of transportation.

Lighthearted young men left the Eastern cities and farms singing a carefree song:

> Oh! California,
>> That's the land for me;
> I'm off for Sacramento
>> With a washbowl on my knee.

Many people had bought a printed map of the gold fields and were convinced that a fortune could be mined with a dishpan and a jackknife. They were to learn about hardship as well.

Some traded their homes for horses. Others bought a seat in an ox-drawn caravan. A few ingenious travelers even put sails on their wagons to catch the prairie wind.

The main route was overland. But travelers soon got over the notion that the cross-country trail was a rainbow with a pot of gold at its western end. The hazards were many. And the roadsides were strewn with the baggage of travelers forced to lighten their loads in order to survive.

Another route was by ship to Panama, and across the jungles of the Isthmus to catch a packet boat on the Pacific side. This proved to be the course of "mud, malaria, and misery." Many turned back.

The most exciting journey of all was "around the Horn" on the most gallant ships afloat. The long voyage to California by way of Cape Horn was made by fast clipper ships in four months. But soon these three-masted, clean-lined craft were straining to beat the latest records.

It was a race for gold. And the drama of it caught the imagination of the world. Currier's lithographs of clipper ships had a lively sale even in England and France.

The grandeur and grace of the Yankee clippers was as poetic as the names on their tapered bows: the *Empress of the Seas* and the *Wild Pigeon,* the *Winged Racer,* and the *Witch of the Wave.*

In New York, crowds thronged to Battery Park to wave farewell as a lofty clipper slid out from its berth, caught the wind in its billowing canvases, and headed majestically for deep water.

Many of the stay-at-homes made a stop at Currier's shop on

Currier & Ives print, "Fashionable 'Turn-outs' in Central Park."

Nassau Street. Newly made lithographs were piled high on out-side tables. For a few cents one could take home a heart-stirring picture of the *Flying Cloud,* a white-winged beauty festooned with tiers of heaving sails.

For many people, the lithograph was a link with adventure. Currier & Ives also found a profitable market for subjects that were close to home and told a simple story. One of the most popular was entitled "The Life of a Hunter—A Tight Fix," and depicted a hunter's encounter with a huge bear. In an attractive country scene called "The Road—Winter," showing a couple sleighing, the models used by the artist were Currier and his wife. Other widely sold prints dealt with life on the prairie and the progress of the railroads, with outdoor sports and the return of hoopskirts to the fashion of the day, with holidays and horse racing. A dramatic picture showed the branding of a slave.

The two partners made a careful record of the subjects and the drawings in greatest demand. The stones for such lithographs were filed on large racks and reprinted again and again whenever the supply ran out. These were indeed precious stones!

The lithography firm had a knack for dramatizing the significant trends in American life. They took note of a new game that was stirring up the dust in cow pastures around New York City.

Baseball in those days was played with thirteen men on a team. The uniforms included pantaloons and straw hats. Often a group of people in the same occupation banded together to form a team. Some of the earliest teams were composed entirely of firemen, school teachers, dairy workers, or clergymen.

Currier & Ives issued a large lithograph showing a lively base-ball game, with a caption reading, "The American National Game of Base Ball." The name took hold and baseball has remained the "national game."

BRANDING SLAVES,

ON THE COAST OF AFRICA PREVIOUS TO EMBARKATION.

Many of the lithographs were taken into backwoods America in the packs of peddlers. These traveling merchants were a common but colorful sight in those years. They carried a wide variety of merchandise such as gunpowder and window glass, calico and kettles. Their trade was among rural folk, mountaineers, miners, and railroad builders.

For the use of the peddlers, Currier & Ives issued a catalogue, advertising that they had "eleven hundred subjects" available in lithographs. They catalogued the prints under such categories as "Juvenile, Domestic, Love Scenes, Kittens and Puppies, Ladies' Heads, Patriotic, Landscapes, Vessels, Comic, School Rewards and Drawing Studies, Flowers and Fruits, Motto Cards, Horses, Family Registers, Memory Pieces and Miscellaneous in great variety, and all elegant and salable Pictures."

The company added that "pictures have now become a necessity, and the price at which they can be retailed is so low that everybody can afford to buy them."

Certainly these prints did seem to fill a need in the life of the times. The lithographs were to be found in the homes of rich and poor, but mostly of those at the middle-income level.

Currier & Ives had a wide variety of artists working for them. And while few of the lithographs could be considered works of art, many were extremely well done, the work of skillful and talented men and women. The artists were largely specialized in particular subjects, some dealing with the outdoor life, others depicting the American home, and still others concentrating on political events.

One of the Currier & Ives artists was Thomas Nast, the cartoonist who created the symbols of the elephant and the donkey for the Republican and Democratic parties. It was Nast who pictured "Uncle Sam" in his patriotic garb—with a strong resemblance to Abraham Lincoln.

The firm of Currier & Ives had avoided taking sides in the

political battles of the day. But as the somber year of 1860 approached, the partners brought their influence to bear on the growing controversy that threatened to erupt into civil war. In a brilliant series of topical prints, cartoons, and posters, they sought to enlighten the public on the issues of slavery and secession.

On a stormy February day in 1860, a towering, roughhewn man entered a photographer's studio on Tenth Street in New York City. He introduced himself as Abraham Lincoln.

The photographer quickly set up his equipment. But his subject was not an easy one. The photographer fussed with the head clamp he used to keep his customers perfectly still. However, Lincoln was six feet, four inches tall, and the clamp was too short.

"Ah," said Lincoln sympathetically, "I see you want to shorten my neck."

"That's just it!" came the reply. Both men laughed.

The photographer was Mathew B. Brady, one of America's pioneers of the camera. His customer was a man not well known in the East. Lincoln was an Illinois congressman, one of many men being discussed as a candidate in the presidential election to be held in the fall of that year.

Brady later remembered all the difficulties he had had with Lincoln's portrait. "I had trouble in making a natural picture," Brady recalled.

Heavy snow was falling as Lincoln left Brady's studio. The tall man headed for the auditorium at Cooper Union. Despite the snowstorm, a large audience awaited his speech.

That night, in clear and sober language, Lincoln summed up the arguments against slavery that he had developed during a long series of Illinois debates with Stephen A. Douglas, his political opponent. Douglas would have people believe, said

Lincoln, "that a horse chestnut is the same as a chestnut horse."

On the platform in the Cooper Union hall, Lincoln faced his audience and extended a gnarled hand. With deep conviction, he stated simply: "Slavery is wrong!"

The crowd stirred to their feet and cheered for the quiet-speaking man from Illinois.

The events in New York City that February day were to change Lincoln's life, and the course of the nation as well. The impact of the Cooper Union speech was to help bring him the nomination for President of the United States. And the Brady portrait was to play a significant part in the election campaign.

After his nomination, Lincoln stayed close to home. In the warm summer days of 1860, the other presidential candidates began their election campaigns. Lincoln had ended his.

The Illinois congressman stated that his stand on the important issues of the day was already "in print and open to all who will read." He made no political speeches, nor did he issue any public statements. He remained in Springfield, Illinois, received a few visitors in his modest house, answered a few letters. It was said that Lincoln did not really run for election; he walked.

Meanwhile, the lithographed posters and cartoons began appearing. Currie & Ives took the photograph by Mathew Brady and made striking campaign posters from it.

The Currier & Ives workshop hummed with election activity. The Lincoln poster was lithographed in several sizes, the presses running night and day. Up on the fifth floor, a group of young women seated at long tables were hand-coloring the Lincoln posters. In the center of each table was a poster which had been painted by an artist. The artisans used this as a model, adding the tints to the black-and-white lithographs by hand.

These lithographs, turned out by the thousands, began appearing in barbershops and taverns, at town meetings and on cross-road signboards all over the nation.

Currier & Ives poster of Lincoln, based on Brady's photograph taken in 1860. (New York Public Library.)

Of the four presidential candidates, the Illinois congressman was probably the least known of all. But the lithographed poster helped to answer the often heard question, "Who is this man Lincoln?"

The opposition tried to fasten on Lincoln the nickname "Old Abe," figuring that such a label would be enough to destroy any man's chances. But the Currier & Ives poster showed that the fifty-one-year-old Lincoln was "not really that old after all."

To the dismay of his opponents, the nickname soon changed to "Honest Old Abe." And strangely enough, Lincoln's foes found that every underhanded blow they struck at him came back at them with double force.

Jeering at Lincoln's humble background, his opponents laughingly called him a "rail splitter." What they failed to realize was that in 1860 America was a nation of rail fences and rail splitters. The phrase only helped to establish Lincoln's kinship with every man who had ever swung an ax.

Currier & Ives issued a series of lithographed cartoons showing Lincoln as the earthy "rail candidate," whose election would prove that the highest office in a democracy is open to the common man.

One of these cartoons showed Lincoln in the setting of the new sport which was then sweeping the country. Lincoln was pictured coming up to bat against his opponents with a fence rail, ready to hit a "home run."

One corrupt political boss, whose long-time practice was to keep the large numbers of foreign-born voters in his district in complete ignorance as to the political issues, threw up his hands in anger when the Currier & Ives cartoons appeared everywhere. "These voters can't read," he cried, "but they sure can't help seeing those pictures."

By arrangement with the photographer, the full-length camera portrait of Lincoln was adapted to many uses. Each lithograph appeared with the inscription, "From a photograph by Mathew Brady."

When Lincoln began growing a beard late in 1860, one of the Currier & Ives artists made some changes on the lithographic stone. With a few deft crayon strokes, a beard was added!

By late fall, the election campaign reached a peak of frenzy. Lincoln's supporters included a lively organization called The Wide Awakes. In towns and villages, their torchlight parades swung jauntily through the streets. They staged bonfires and barbecues, carrying the familiar Lincoln posters and banners under the slogan "Lincoln and Liberty."

Election night found Lincoln in his home town, in the tiny telegraph office down near the railroad tracks. It was after midnight when the chattering telegraph instrument spelled out victory.

The small-town streets were quiet and the prairie wind whipped a campaign banner with the portrait of the man who was now President-elect.

"I guess I'll go home now," said Lincoln, and he strode long-legged toward the plain little house where he lived with his family.

At a Washington gathering, months later, Lincoln and some friends were chatting about the recent election and the effectiveness of the poster that Currier & Ives had made from a photograph. The President-elect introduced one of his invited guests, the photographer Mathew B. Brady. Said Lincoln: "Brady and the Cooper Union speech made me President."

Brady went on to make a remarkable camera record of the Civil War, a series of pictures that brought home to the world the full human tragedy of armed conflict. Often working under fire, Brady carried his unwieldy equipment into the smoldering battlefields. He traveled by means of a wagon equipped with a darkroom for developing his pictures.

Brady's camera disclosed the bloodshed at Bull Run and all the horror of Gettysburg. Never before had a set of photographs revealed so dramatically the power of the camera to depict news events.

With the coming of photography, there were some who predicted the decline of lithography. What they failed to foresee was the firm partnership which was already forming between these two crafts.

7

Light on Stone

With remarkable foresight, Aloys Senefelder was able to predict many features of the future course of lithography. But one development was beyond the imagination of lithography's mastermind in Munich. It was based on the bold idea that an image on stone could be made by the action of light.

This was the thought that occurred to the French chemist Joseph Nicéphore Niepce. Niepce was a member of a well-to-do family, living on a comfortable estate in the vineyard region near Chalon. In 1815, at the age of fifty, Niepce came home at last from his long military service. The exhausting Napoleonic campaigns were over, and Niepce could turn his creative mind to constructive things.

When Aloys Senefelder was at work on his book explaining lithography, Niepce had already experimented with this printing process and had become a skillful artisan on stone.

As he worked on his lithographs, the play of sunlight and shadow set him thinking. He wondered if "nature might be persuaded to draw its own portrait" on the stone.

For ages it had been observed that sunlight filtering through a pinhole into a dark room can produce a startling effect; an inverse image of the scene outside may flash upon the interior wall opposite the pinhole. Another natural occurrence had also been noted—that some chemical substances become darker and others harden when exposed to light rays.

Several inventors had made attempts to use these two phenomena to create a photograph, a stable picture made naturally by light rays. It was Joseph Niepce who helped to show the world how to achieve this result.

The Frenchman took an old jewel box and fitted it with a lens. Inside was a paper coated with a substance sensitive to light.

Niepce completed this camera in the early spring. And each day he scanned the skies, anxious for the return of a more radiant sun. One bright April morning, he set up the little apparatus on a window sill. For the next eight hours he waited while the sun crossed overhead.

By nightfall, he had a photograph—one in which dark objects appeared light and the daytime sky was dark. But in plain view on the paper was the scene from the attic window!

Niepce sent off his exciting news to his brother Claude in Paris: "I saw on the white paper all the part of the birdhouse seen from the window and a faint image of the casement. . . . The possibility of painting in this way seems to me almost demonstrated."

Like Niepce, other inventors had achieved a crude photograph, but the image was a will-o'-the-wisp that refused to stay put. During a few agonizing moments, the picture gradually faded, and finally vanished.

Many were experimenting in a determined effort to fix the image permanently. For Niepce, the challenge went even further. His idea was to entrap the image on a lithographic stone—and use the stone to print copies.

There are many light-sensitive chemicals that can be used to coat a photographic plate. But Niepce was looking for a greasy substance which would lend itself to the technique of lithography. He experimented, for example, with oily minerals known as asphalt or bitumen, which turn hard when exposed to light.

One day Niepce coated a polished pewter plate with bitumen. On top of it he placed a black-and-white drawing printed on transparent paper. After hours in the sun, the bitumen coating had hardened wherever light could penetrate the blank spaces on the paper. Niepce washed away the unhardened portions of coating. What he had left was a negative contact print on the pewter plate.

Niepce was frustrated by the fact that he could only produce a picture in which the dark and light portions of the scene were reversed—the kind of image called a negative. Later it was learned that by a simple method a negative on glass or film can be used to make one or more positives, with the light and dark tones restored to their true appearance.

In his experiments, Niepce came quite close to making a photographic image which could be used for lithographic printing. However, he died in 1833 thinking that he had failed.

The man who inherited Niepce's problem was another Frenchman, a civil engineer named Alphonse Louis Poitevin whose work had ranged from running a glassworks in Alsace to managing silver mines in North Africa. Somehow, he found a greater challenge in lithography.

He searched, as had Niepce, for a light-sensitive substance receptive to the greasy ink which is used in lithography. Niepce had used pitch and tar. Poitevin tried eggs.

One day he discovered a coating which solved the problem. It was made by combining certain chemicals with albumen from the whites of eggs. When exposed to light, this coating hardened in a much shorter time than bitumen. By exposing a coated stone surface under a photographic negative on a translucent material, the image could be permanently captured on the stone. The unhardened portions of the coating, Poitevin found, could be washed away with water. When he applied a roller of greasy ink over the wet stone, the photographic image showed up black and glistening.

Poitevin was not skilled in lithography. But he sought out help in a small Paris shop where there were workmen expert in making fine prints from stone. Poitevin's prints caused a stir in Paris, where many thought that Poitevin's methods could someday be used to produce excellent printed matter of all kinds in large quantities. Others were dismayed that this process would lose the very qualities for which lithography was famous. Copies made from a hard albumen coating would be much different from those produced from an artist's crayon drawing. A print from a crayon image has a rich range of tones from deep black to delicate grays, but the light-hardened albumen could print only one tone—black.

What saved these early experiments from complete failure was the grainy texture of the stone. The porous lithographer's limestone has a surface made up of tiny hills and valleys. A photographic image printed from such a surface will not appear as harsh black and white, but will in fact give the illusion of some of the in-between gray tones of the photograph.

However, it was many years before the real solution to the problem reduced itself to the size of a tiny dot.

In the 1880s, newspapers began printing their first photographs. These pictures were made up of thousands of evenly spaced black dots. Through a magnifying glass, it could be seen that the light-gray tones in the photograph were made up of the smallest dots. The dark-gray tones were clusters of larger dots running together.

This method of capturing the in-between grays of the photograph was called the halftone process. The simple piece of equipment used to achieve this result was a piece of glass, etched with two sets of black lines, closely and evenly spaced, at right angles to each other.

Detail of Daumier's "The Legislative Belly," shown in inset, is greatly magnified to reveal the pattern of dots producing the various shades of black and gray in a halftone photograph.

When the image was photographed through this finely meshed screen, it was broken up into thousands of smaller and larger dots. In print, the halftone photograph gives the illusion of gray tones, even though the picture is made up entirely of individual black dots on white paper.

The discovery of a practical method of printing photographs had a startling effect on all branches of the printing industry. The three established methods of commercial printing—letterpress, gravure, and lithography—were drawn into sharp rivalry.

Letterpress, long predominant in newspaper printing, was in the forefront in developing the new halftone process. Gravure was not far behind. Lithography lagged—but not for long.

Competing for higher quality in printed photographs proved to be a matter of using finer and finer screens in order to achieve greater detail, a wider range of tones, a better blend of smaller dots. As it turned out, lithography was able to produce the finest dot of all.

The great innovations of the nineteenth century linked people together across time and distance. Inventors produced the telgraph and telephone, the steam engine and steamboat. The era extended the range of human communication. The printing industry speeded the flow of words, displayed brilliant images, and splashed color on the printed page.

It was a time that wedded laboratory science to factory technology. And color printing was developed by an interesting combination of scientists, artists, and printers.

As a boy in Scotland, James Clerk Maxwell had been filled with wonder to hold a glass prism to the sun's rays. Fascinated by the dazzling beauty of the spectrum, he was also curious about the nature of light and color.

Maxwell, who was to become one of the greatest physicists of all time, gave some of his attention to the study of color. He investigated the way in which light is reflected from an opaque surface and observed by the human eye.

In college, Maxwell returned to the colorful spinning top of his childhood. He fitted his top with colored disks which could be varied in size. When the top was spinning rapidly, the colors on the disks merged into a new color.

His tests led him to a set of mathematical formulas for mixing opaque color such as paint or ink. Beginning with the three primary colors, he accurately determined the combinations and proportions necessary to produce the entire range of colors.

By the 1880s the colored top, which Maxwell called a "teetotum," found its way to Paris and into the studios of a group of artists who were absorbed with the problems of color. These painters had turned to science to discover how to capture on canvas the impression of light.

Georges Seurat spent much of his time studying the scientific journals on the theory of color and spinning the teetotum. In his large paintings of scenes in the Paris parks, Seurat displayed a new technique that created a sensation. With the point of his brush, he built up his images from tiny dots of color placed side by side.

Seurat's technique gave a luminous, shimmering quality to his works. This kind of painting is called "pointillism." It laid the basis for other important experiments by artists of the period with color and light.

In the early 1890s, the Paris art center became excited about another artist, whose lithographs showed a brash and brilliant use of color. He was Henri Toulouse-Lautrec, a strange little man newly arrived in Paris.

When he was fourteen years old, Lautrec had slipped from a chair and broken his thigh bone. The leg had failed to mend properly, and gradually it became clear that the boy had an incurable bone disease. His legs stopped growing.

"Aristide Bruant," by Toulouse-Lautrec.
(Metropolitan Museum of Art.)

Henri's days of vigorous activity, of horsemanship and other outdoor sports, were over. His immense vitality was poured into creative work. Among his many important art works are thousands of lithographs—in color.

Lautrec used the greasy crayon with sureness and speed. And

lithography seemed to be the perfect medium for his art. He was able to draw directly on the stone without making any kind of preliminary sketch. Like many of the other artists of the time who were devoted to lithography, he worked with the artisans who made the finished prints on a hand press.

One of Lautrec's pictures on stone shows the lithography workshop in Paris where so many of his prints were made. It depicts the stone in the press, the bowl for dampening the stone, the pots of colored ink, an elderly craftsman in shirt sleeves turning the hand crank, and a young woman examining the first proof.

Lautrec turned his great talent to designing vivid lithographed posters. They appeared everywhere. Paris, "the City of Light," was set ablaze with Lautrec's colors. His eye-catching advertisements reflected the spirit of Montmartre. Like the mode of life in this artists' quarter, they were colorful, bizarre, and carefree.

Lautrec did not confine himself to drawing with the lithographic crayon; he also painted directly on the stone with greasy ink to achieve a brushwork effect, or sometimes applied it in broad strokes with a palette knife. In some of his posters unusual color harmonies were created by spattering the ink on the stone.

For this latter technique the three large stones that would be used to print the three colors of the finished poster were prepared in the usual fashion. In accordance with his design, Lautrec covered certain areas of each stone with a protective paper shield. Then he filled a stiff-bristled toothbrush with the greasy ink and scraped across the bristles with a knife to throw a fine spray of the ink onto the exposed parts of the stone. Thus, the image on each stone was made up of a stipple of dots.

In printing the poster a single color of printing ink was used for each stone. The finished poster, with its colored dots blended together, had a novel range of subtle tints.

The clustering of many-colored dots was precisely the pattern applied soon after in the printing of photographs in full color, and subsequently it was adapted to color reproduction in modern lithographic presses.

A journeyman printer from Ithaca, New York, named Frederic E. Ives was a pioneer in the effort to find a method of color printing based on photography. Ives had made his first important contribution in the development of the halftone screen in the 1880s.

He went on to devise a practical color camera. This camera took three pictures at once, each recording one of the three primary colors in the scene on which the camera was focused. The three images were then superimposed to form a single full-color photograph.

Ives's research soon led him to a workable process of three-color printing. The basic methods of color printing today combine the principles and techniques on which Ives spent a long and productive lifetime. They apply the science of color and light to the art of color printing.

A colored picture is reproduced by laying a series of ink images on paper which, when seen in combination, will re-create the colors that appeared in the original.

The basic process begins by making three exposures of the original picture to obtain the so-called color-separation negatives. Each exposure is made through a different color filter that lets the shades of only one of the three primary colors reach the film. When developed, each of the three negatives is a record of one of the three component colors in the original picture.

In order to get the fine detail on paper, it is necessary for each of these three photographic records to be broken down into dots by means of the halftone screen. A set of printing plates is then made from the films. On the press, each of these plates is used with a colored ink. As the paper goes through the press, it is printed separately from each of the three plates. Each plate lays down its image in color in the form of a pattern of colored dots.

The process that began by separating the colors now brings them back together again on the printed page. The result is a color-printed picture very much like the original. Seen through a magnifying glass, such color printing appears as clustered red, blue, and yellow dots of varying sizes, the dots arranged in "rosette" patterns, side by side.

It was in the late 1890s that the methods of color lithography by photographic means were developed. However, there were many years of experimentation and research before the process was refined. Better camera techniques and equipment had to be devised. The colored inks had to be improved. A black plate was added to obtain strength in detail and more gray tones. In fine work, additional color plates were used.

The development of photographic processes further emphasized the two distinct trends of lithography—as an industrial technique and as an art medium.

The camera could copy. The camera could duplicate any image set before it. In this commercial form, lithography no longer depended directly on the creative artist.

On the other hand, lithography remained an important art medium. Artists continued to use the original method of drawing directly on stone, to devote themselves to the special kind of fine art work which is known as print-making, as distinct from printing.

Each of us carries around the means for making a kind of "print." The flat hand, pressed against a smooth surface, will produce a handprint merely from the natural oils of the skin.

In a sense, the artist's lithograph is such a print. It is the personal mark of the creative artist recorded on the sensitive stone. Today, as in the past, the artist finds lithography to be a faithful medium through which to express himself.

8

The Art of Print-making

"The art of lithography has spread even to Philadelphia!" It was in 1816 that Aloys Senefelder noted down this fact with joy and amazement.

Today the art of lithography is taught to the young people of Philadelphia in a novel fashion. A truck makes a tour of all the city's schools. A complete press is unloaded and wheeled into the classroom. The students are then treated to a demonstration by artists of how a lithograph is made from stone.

The classes are also shown how other kinds of fine prints are made, including woodcuts, engravings, and etchings. The finished print made by each medium has a particular "look" all its own.

As the students watch this graphic exhibition, one fact is made very clear—there is a direct link between the artist himself and the print in its final form. The demonstration shows the major difference between the artist's fine print and a machine-printed reproduction which may be turned out in thousands of copies by a commercial process.

A reproduction may begin with an oil-color painting by a famous artist. By means of photography, the painting is copied, its colors separated by camera filters and reduced to halftone dots. Plates are made and the colored images are reunited in the actual printing.

The final product may be a good likeness of the original oil painting. However, no amount of industrial technique or modern machinery can replace the artist himself. If a factory-made reproduction were examined under a strong magnifying glass for traces of the artist's handiwork, one would see nothing but masses of halftone dots. The manufacture of such a reproduction clearly does not involve the artist himself, and it is not considered a work of art.

In contrast, the artist's fine print is his own creation from beginning to end. Each print is his own work as much as an oil painting or a water color made by his own hand.

The artist makes his plate of metal, wood, or stone. In the case of the lithograph, the artist sometimes spends hours preparing the surfaces of his stones. Each one is ground and grained according to his desires. The old image is painstakingly removed by rubbing stone against stone until a flat, clean surface is achieved. The grain of the limestone, which holds the grease drawing and entraps the water film in blank areas, also gives the print the velvety quality characteristic of the lithograph.

The artist may be assisted by an artisan in transferring the image to the plate for an etching or an engraving, or in operating the press. But it is the artist who selects the colors, the inks, and the paper. And the prints themselves are made by him or under his supervision.

In print-making, the first impression is not necessarily the best. The artist carefully selects only those prints that achieve the effect he wants. The approved impressions are rigidly limited in quantity, and ordinarily the plate or the image on the stone is then destroyed. The prints are usually numbered and signed by the artist. Each one is considered an original work of art.

Several years ago, separate exhibitions of artists' fine prints opened on the same day in sixteen American cities. Each museum showed exactly the same collection of fine prints—all of them originals.

The fine woodcuts and engravings that appeared in fifteenth-century Europe played an important role in the popular awakening which changed the conditions of life across the Western world.

Up to that time, the enjoyment of art was largely restricted to the wealthy and powerful, who were the patrons of the painters and sculptors. Few people could afford an original oil painting; but the fine print could be owned by many more.

The popularity of the fine print reflected the widening desire among people for the better things of life that was a part of their growing struggle for democracy.

The artist found that he could reach a wide and appreciative audience. Often he divided his time between painting in oils for his rich patrons and making prints from plates for the public.

Such an artist was Francisco Goya. At the very time that Senefelder was inventing lithography in Munich, Goya had achieved prominence as chief court artist in Madrid.

From a humble background, Goya had risen to become the portrait painter of the Spanish nobility. And yet, the artist resented the corruption he saw around him.

Lithograph made by Goya when he was 77 years old. (New York Public Library.)

While the eighteenth century drew to a close, Goya turned to making fine prints. His prints satirized the harsh tyranny and the religious persecution of his time. Goya was not a great reformer. But in his prints, which dealt mainly with the conditions of life in Spain, he expressed a deep sympathy for his fellow man.

As a palace painter, he used canvas and oils. As a social critic, he used paper and ink to produce large numbers of superb prints

on the disasters of war, revealing the senseless brutality of the battlefield.

In voluntary exile in France, when he was close to eighty years old, Goya learned of a new print medium for expressing his ideas. He began to work in lithography.

The aged artist propped the stone up on a painter's easel and used the crayons as though they were brushes. He finished his

Daumier's lithograph "Nadar Elevating Photography to a High Art," published in 1862, lampooned an early photographer who took his camera up in a balloon to obtain aerial photographs of Paris. (George Eastman House.)

work by using a scraper on the stone to bring out the high lights.

Far from the Spanish court, he set to work with great zeal on a series of lithographs. Goya was feeble and half blind. "I lack everything," he said. "Only my will survives."

Among Goya's lithographs was a magnificent series showing the drama of the bull ring. These prints, done in the year 1825, were the first great masterpieces in lithography.

In the capable hands of Honoré Daumier, lithography became even more responsive to the artist's will. In Daumier's prints, the full range of lithography was put into play.

Early in his life, he had experimented with engravings, etchings, and woodcuts. However, he found these methods wanting. For one thing, with these relief methods, the artist often had to depend on craftsmen to do the final cutting of the plate.

"I find that the lithographic crayon alone follows my thought," Daumier told his friends, "and only by this method can I be certain of getting a faithful copy of what I have drawn."

For Daumier, work on the stone always seemed more direct than other kinds of print-making. The artist does not need to wait for a press proof to be made before he can see what he has done. The drawing is always visible. It grows as he works.

Daumier found that lithography offered him a broad variety of textures and tones. He used his crayon to achieve the drama of strong black-and-white contrasts. He could attain soft shadings. The stone surface permitted the most delicate handling of the human form and face.

Encouraged by Daumier's example, many of the great artists of his age turned to lithography. Masterpieces done on stone appeared with the signatures of Manet, Renoir, Cezanne, van Gogh.

Among the outstanding American lithographers at the beginning of the twentieth century was George Bellows. While at college, Bellows excelled in athletics and almost made a career of baseball as a shortstop.

Instead he became an artist, and many of his vigorous works reflect his interest in sports. Bellows drew the bustling scenes of life in New York City. He also conveyed great tenderness in the lithographic portrait of his young daughter Jean, one of his favorite subjects.

His lithographs revealed the qualities that could be achieved with what Bellows called "a stick of grease." He captured the silvery play of light and shade. With bold strokes on the stone, he built powerful patterns. In these lithographs can be seen the perfect unity of the artist and his medium.

It was only late in his short life that Bellows "discovered" lithography. With great delight he told his friends of his excitement at drawing on large stones and evolving his own methods

George Bellows' lithograph of a crucial moment in the Dempsey-Firpo prize fight. (Metropolitan Museum of Art.)

of work. Bellows stirred many artists to a new interest in working on stone at a time when other techniques had momentarily put lithography into the background.

The lithographic method has repeatedly attained great popularity as some brilliant lithographer revealed anew the beauty and power, the highly individual expression, that could be achieved on the stone. It was this aspect of lithography that appealed greatly to Pablo Picasso.

From his early years as an artist, Picasso took an interest in the various kinds of print-making. One of his first efforts showed a bull-ring performer. When he saw the finished print the artist realized, to his chagrin, that he had failed to reverse his design on the plate, so that the figure in the print appeared holding a lance in the wrong hand. Picasso broke into laughter and promptly retitled his print "Left-handed Picador."

"Profile on a Black Background," lithograph made by Picasso on March 3, 1947. The date appears in reverse, as the artist forgot to write backward on the stone. (New York Public Library.)

Like Goya a century before him, the Spanish-born Picasso returned again and again to the subject of the bull ring, which seemed to reflect the life of the common people of Spain.

In the late 1940s Picasso returned to lithography with great enthusiasm, producing a large number of brilliant color prints. During those years, he could usually be found in the Paris lithography workshop of the Mourlot brothers. Picasso often worked there from early dawn until late at night perfecting his techniques. Many of his lithographs were drawn on a type of paper that was specially coated so that the design could be easily transferred to stone.

It was the need to set down ideas with great speed and vigor that attracted Picasso and other artists to lithography, which has maintained its high level of importance as an art medium. New prints are being created. Older ones are eagerly sought by the public.

Although few of them are considered to have much artistic merit, even the old Currier & Ives prints are in great demand. In a recent year, a Currier & Ives print which originally sold for a few coins was bought for several thousand dollars.

Of widespread interest are the prints from the earliest years of lithography, when the impressions from the stone varied widely in quality and usage. While some lithographs were art masterpieces, others served everyday needs. From the old-fashioned presses came handbills and calendars, posters and postcards. Some lithographs were as plain as a train schedule. Others were as vivid as a valentine.

In his unforgettable *Christmas Carol*, the British author Charles Dickens described the holiday spirit of London in an earlier day. Dickens' famous story of Scrooge and the Cratchit family was published in 1843.

A bright lithographed card appeared in London that same year.

The first Christmas card, published in London by Horsley in 1843.

It was the work of John Colcott Horsley. This was the first Christmas card.

Horsley's card showed several scenes—a British family enjoying their Christmas dinner, and also sharing their bounty with the poor. The idea of Christmas cards caught on immediately. However, they were considered at the time to be a pleasant but passing fad. That early lithographed greeting, the first Christmas card, was produced in an edition of one thousand copies. Today some seven billion greeting cards are produced in America each year, the bulk of them pouring from lithography presses. No one could have guessed what a widespread custom and a giant industry were being born on that Christmas of 1843.

It was not too many years afterward that the first lithographed valentines appeared, also in England. Mid-February had long been marked as the time of wooing among birds. And young men chose this date to serenade their ladies and express their feelings in ardent messages and tender verse.

When British lithographers began putting out gay colored cards, they caught the fancy of young people. The exchanging of valentines, sentimental or comic, has become a hearty tradition.

In America, the greeting-card industry flourished with the help of men such as Louis Prang, a Boston lithographer who became known for his outstanding craftsmanship during the latter decades of the nineteenth century. Prang was noted for the excellent drawing, design, and coloring of his greeting cards, which were usually printed in eight colors. There were some cards on which Prang used as many as twenty lithographic stones to achieve the color combinations he desired.

The practice of sending greeting cards has grown steadily in popularity. The important events of people's lives—births, marriages, anniversaries, and holidays—are heralded by attractive lithographed cards.

As the nineteenth century drew to a close, lithography was coming of age as an industry. Across America, there were more and more lithography shops. They became less specialized in the kind of work they produced, more versatile in many varieties of printing. There were more skilled craftsmen. The techniques were changing.

Commercial lithography raced ahead to meet the twentieth century. The cumbersome stone was replaced by a light, thin, metal plate. The main instrument used to make the image was no longer the crayon but the camera. The press, motor-driven, took on the circular shape of speed.

9

Words and Pictures

The "stone age" of commercial lithography ended quietly. In the early years of this century, the industry turned to using thin metal plates. The reasons were clear.

As the size of printed sheets became larger, suitable stones were more expensive and harder to handle. More important, the newer and faster lithography presses were designed on the principle of two spinning cylinders, with the white paper wrapped around one cylinder and the thin metal plate wrapped around the other.

And yet, the Bavarian limestone still played an important role in the industry. Whatever materials were later used, metals and plastics, they were made to simulate the surface qualities of the

A lithographic plate is being fastened onto a modern press.

stone. To accomplish this, the metal is put through a strange ordeal. An aluminum or zinc plate is laid in a shallow basin. Large quantities of steel marbles are poured on the surface of the plate, along with water and sandy abrasives. The entire basin is continuously vibrated, the balls grinding the sand against the metal surface of the plate. After lengthy treatment, the plate has a uniformly roughened texture, a grain similar to that of the lithographer's limestone.

Before the plate is ready to take an image, it is evenly covered with a light-sensitive coating. The plate is now placed in contact with a film negative, which bears the image to be printed. It is then exposed to strong light that passes through the clear portions of the negative and hardens the coating beneath, making it insoluble in water.

The plate is then ready for developing—which consists mainly of washing away the remnants of unhardened coating. Then the image is topped with greasy ink. As for the nonimage area, it is chemically treated so that it will hold a film of water and thus remain free of any trace of ink.

Once on the press, the plate is dampened with water before inking rollers cross its surface. Chemically the two liquids, water and greasy ink, reject each other. Each remains in its place. Only the grease-covered image, made up of the lines of type and the halftone dots of photographs, accepts the ink. And with each turn of the press, the words and pictures are imprinted on paper.

Stone has always been a symbol of something durable. But in lithography, metal has proved to be longer-lasting stuff. There are plates which can produce a million impressions and more.

At the same time that the metal plate was being developed, a revolution in press design was also in the making.

In Nutley, New Jersey, in the year 1904, the printer Ira Rubel was operating his old-fashioned stone press while a woman worker fed sheets of paper onto the cylinder. By accident she missed one turn of the motor-driven press, and the stone transferred an inky image to the bare rubber surface of the revolving cylinder. When the young lady fed the next sheet of paper into the press, the image printed on both sides of the paper.

Rubel stopped the press. He wanted a second look at the "spoiled" sheet. He put his magnifying glass to the images on the front and back of the sheet of paper. To his amazement, the impression on the back, transferred from the rubber, was even clearer and cleaner than that made directly from the stone. In that moment, the idea of "offset" lithography was born.

Rubel set to work designing a new press. It was to have an extra cylinder, covered with a rubber blanket.

Rubel's press borrowed some improvements from presses which were being used to print the lithographic image on metal. It had some new features as well. As the press turned, the inked image was transferred to the cylinder covered with a rubber blanket. In turn, the ink-wet image was relayed, or "offset," to the paper sheet.

The offset method proved to have some important advantages. For one thing, it did away with many of the old problems that resulted when the damp plate came into direct contact with the paper.

The soft rubber blanket was also capable of impressing the image clearly on types of paper which have a rough surface. In fact, the new press offered greater possibilities for printing on metal and many other materials.

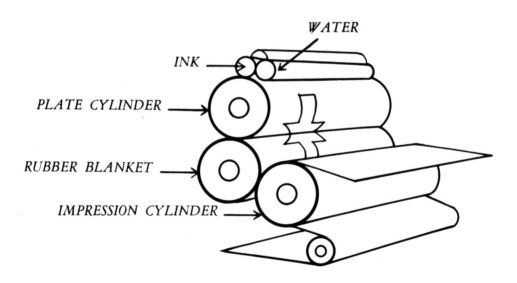

The rubber "offset" cylinder bearing the inked image in reverse transfers the impression onto paper passing through the press.

Offset printing meant less wear and tear on the plate, with the result that plates could be used for longer press runs before the image wore out.

Probably the most important factor of all in the change to offset lithography was that good quality work could be produced at lower cost.

Offset presses today vary greatly in size and speed. The press may print only one color. Or it may be a six-color giant, which is like six presses in one. It may feed automatically from a pile of paper. It may print sheets of metal which will eventually be made into containers. Or it may be a web press, producing books or newspapers from an unwinding roll of paper.

In any case, the press run is the final dramatic showdown. Here unfolds the climax to what may be months of preparatory work by designers, artists, cameramen, "strippers," and platemakers. It is up to the pressman to make a good impression for the whole lithographic process.

The craft of the pressman consists in watching a great many details at once. The job of preparing a press run is called make-ready. This includes the positioning of the many plates so that each color will print in the proper place, in perfect register. The pressman carefully balances the flow of the two fluids from their fountains, so that the ink and water are evenly distributed on the plate. The pressman checks the image as it goes from plate to blanket and from blanket to paper.

The large and complex presses do much more than print. On many, the freshly printed paper goes through a dryer. There are complicated machines built into the press which must be adjusted for proper cutting, perforating, slitting, gathering, folding, stacking, and bundling.

Carefully, every detail is checked. The first finished copies come from the press and get a final "O.K." It is then that the pressman hits the high-speed button.

The swift flow begins. The written word becomes a torrent of printed language. The single picture is repeated a thousandfold in the surging stream from the press.

Printed matter pours out into the modern world in an endless variety of forms, in a deluge of products.

Lithography enters many phases of modern daily life. Road maps and trading stamps are produced by lithography. Advertising folders, display posters, catalogues, and packages are a huge and growing part of this industry.

Today's supermarket is a dazzling display of lithography. Tin cans and cosmetic tubes, moisture-proof boxes and multihued bottle caps, plastic containers and gummed labels—many show the bright designs which are a specialty of offset printing.

In recent years, the lithography industry has grown rapidly. In part, this is due to the readiness of the industry to keep pace with the times. Its craftsmen welcome new improvements in technology, learn new skills, and adopt new methods. In every large city in America, schools have been set up to train both apprentices and journeymen in the latest techniques.

However, commercial printing is shared by the three processes—letterpress, gravure, and lithography. And each has its own specialties. Each has certain advantages in quality and cost, depending on the job to be done.

Each process is particularly suited for certain types of work. Some of the finest magazine printing of all is done today by gravure, and printed money has long been a specialty of this process.

As for letterpress, it has great versatility. Although among the smaller daily and weekly newspapers there is a trend today toward offset lithography, it is not likely that the big city daily newspapers will soon turn away from long-established letterpress methods.

Printing in the Western world began with the letterpress method, when men first cast letters into metal type and used it in a screw-type press.

Gradually, the methods of making type from molten lead were improved. Machinery took over many of the laborious chores of type-making and typesetting. By the middle of the nineteenth century, this so-called hot type was being cast by machines. Complicated inventions were developed which automatically poured hot lead into molds and delivered whole lines of type at a time.

Such molded type has been the source of the printed word for lithography as well as for letterpress and gravure. And even when it turned to photographic methods, commercial lithography continued to depend on hot type.

Once the type was set, the lithographer secured his necessary copy of the text on film by one of two methods. Either he made an inked proof from the type and photographed this proof, or else he could photograph the type itself. But in both cases the text had to be set in metal type before a photographic image could be obtained.

Today, lithography has begun to turn away from its dependence on the metals and molds essential for letterpress printing. Hot type is gradually giving way to "cold type"—which in the traditional sense is not type at all!

So-called cold type is produced by a photographic box which is usually operated by a keyboard. When the keys are punched, individual letters imprinted on film are selected and photographed consecutively from a master set of letters. What emerges from the box are strips of reading matter on film or paper. These strips can be fastened into place to make up blocks or pages of text. The word images can be positioned alongside picture images—and such units are then ready for the photographic steps leading to platemaking.

In its simplest form, the cold-type machine works like an electric typewriter. The more complex equipment in use today has all the amazing functions of the electronic computer.

A continuous stream of words may be fed into such a machine. What emerges is the finished reading matter, set in any desired style of type, arranged in orderly columns, paragraphs, pages. The right-hand margins are perfectly aligned. Within each line, the computer has properly spaced out the letters and words. When a word has to be hyphenated and carried over to the next line, the storage unit of the computer, which contains a complete word list, provides the means for splitting the word in the proper place.

Another development of today is the scanner, an electronic device used in reproducing pictures in full color. By means of a moving camera eye, the scanner can make its way across a many-colored transparent image and automatically produce a set of films with the colors separated for multicolor lithography.

The miracle of electronics also makes it possible to transmit type and picture messages across long distances—or to punch a continuous tape which can later be used to produce the images necessary for lithographic platemaking.

Such inventions open up vast new vistas for lithography, since anything can be reproduced which is put before a camera. As a method of printing pictures in black and white or in color, lithography has always held its own. But in printing combinations of pictures and words, it excels. Often, both illustrations and text are photographed from a single black-and-white copy, and printed as a single unit. One thin metal plate may include photographs, tints, linework, type—everything.

The lithographer, long adept with pictures, has now become extremely handy with words. And the ease with which he combines illustrations and text has put him into the very center of the world-wide boom in books.

The screened positive film is stripped into a master form containing all the art and type to appear on the printed sheet.

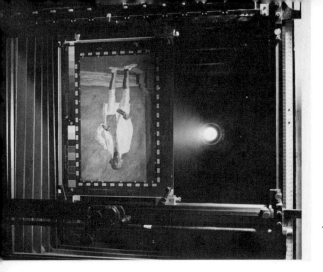

Four-color separations are made on black-and-white film, one for each of the colors, yellow, red, blue, and black, in the original photograph.

Each color-separation negative is then retouched by hand before it is screened in a camera which will produce the color-separation positive.

The size of the dots on the developed film positive will vary with the amount of light that passes through the grid.

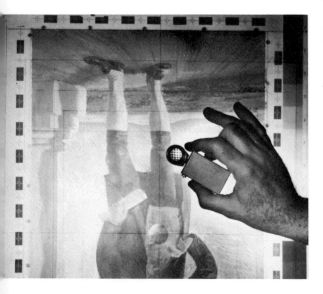

After being exposed to light through a screened positive, the plate is then developed, and a grease-receptive lacquer is applied that adheres only to the image areas, thus making them water-repellant.

This book is a sample of the modern lithographer's skill. At one stage in its preparation, it was in the form of a large number of small pieces of film, each one a camera record of an illustration or a portion of the text. Working over a large glass-topped table lighted from below, a lithographer "stripped" these pieces of film into place.

When he was through with his work, the stripper had completed a series of large "flats," each with a spread of thirty-two pages of the book in film form. These were then ready for the platemaker and the pressman.

At the same time, the book jacket was being prepared for the four-color press. Beginning with the artist's design, the cameraman separated the colors in the book-jacket design and prepared a set of halftone films. In one of the most painstaking of all lithographic operations, these films were checked for the proper size of the dots so that the desired combination of printed colors would be achieved. Where necessary, the dots could be slightly enlarged or reduced in size through the lithographer's skill.

The process of making this book involved mounting the plates on the press with great precision so that each image would print in place. From a set of first proofs, the entire job was checked to see that the pages would be in sequence after the folding and cutting machines had prepared the sheaves of printed pages for the bindery.

At every stage, the lithographers worked from a "dummy," which is the book designer's handmade preview of how the finished book should look.

Through lithography, young people have access today to a rich range of books in their homes and libraries. One of the earliest illustrated books prepared specifically for the enjoyment of young people was Edward Lear's *A Book of Nonsense*, which was published in 1846. The book, written and illustrated by a young British artist and lithographer, gained immediate success.

Lear, who was for a time Queen Victoria's art teacher, presented an odd picture as he arrived each day at London's Buckingham Palace. He was a large, oval-shaped man, with an enormous black beard that reminded people of the bearskin hats worn by the palace guards. Doors opened for him as he made his way through the royal palace to the suite of the young queen. Although Lear was never able to inspire any royal artistic talent, he did keep Queen Victoria amused with his fantastic little sketches.

In spite of his unhappy life, or perhaps because of it, Lear's specialty was comic drawings and hilarious verses to match. When he ran out of nonsense words, Lear manufactured his own.

When *A Book of Nonsense* appeared, it caused quite a stir. Nothing quite like it had ever been seen. The book was completely lithographed, pictures and poetry. And it set a pattern in children's literature for generations to come.

Since its earliest days, lithography and bookmaking have been associated—largely through the work on stone of great illustrators.

Some of the best-known artists of the nineteenth and twentieth centuries have lithographed illustrations for books. These include many of the great classics, issued in fine editions.

At the same time, modern lithography has helped make books plentiful and readily available, supplementing readable text with colorful drawings, designs, and photographs.

Today there is a new and growing interest in books. The printing presses of the earth have been put into vigorous service in response to the popular demand for reading matter of almost every kind. The result has been an outpouring of books by the billions that are easy to handle, easy to read—and easy on the purse.

In America, more and better textbooks have made the teacher's work more effective and the pupil's life more interesting. Nine out of every ten school books are lithographed. And the advantage of lithography as a printing method grows as more pictures are added and more colors are used.

A page from the original edition (1864) of A Book of Nonsense.

There was a Young Lady whose bonnet,   came untied when the birds sate upon it;
But she said, " I don't care !   all the birds in the air
Are welcome to sit on my bonnet !"

5

In some of the newly developing countries of Asia and Africa, publishing industries are now being established. Many of the new plants have offset lithography presses. The equipment is often simpler and less costly to operate than that needed for the older forms of printing. Offset book-publishing plants can operate without expensive type or hot-metal equipment or the many rigid limitations of letterpress and gravure printing.

These offset presses are beginning to meet the need for illustrated books in newly opened schoolrooms and in classes where adults are being taught how to read. Vast numbers of books in many languages are being put into the hands of new readers.

Whereas hand-carved stones once helped to light the way of learning from one generation to the next, Senefelder's use of stone has, in quite another way, brought enlightenment to the lands of the ancient stone-carvers. Where the artisan once hacked his solitary record into a stone slab, the modern lithographer today supplies copies of a message to millions of readers.

In central America, Indians once carved into a huge tablet a marvelous calendar which recorded the history, myths, and prophecies of the Mayan civilization. Today in this region, the illustrated book is helping to end illiteracy in tribal villages and rural areas. Lithographed materials are raising the levels of learning and living.

Near the mouth of the Nile, Napoleon's soldiers found a stone, the Rosetta stone, carved with an inscription in three different kinds of writing. That stone proved to be the key which revealed the meaning of ancient Egyptian hieroglyphics that had remained a mystery for centuries.

Today in the Middle East, school children learn modern languages, as well as the tongues spoken by their forebears. Their textbooks are produced by modern lithographic presses in the cities of Cairo and Jerusalem.

To this day, engraved tablets still bear the writings of Confucius. But new generations of students no longer rely on stone carvings or stone rubbings. In Asia, where printing began, the output of books still lags behind the need. But offset presses are being installed in growing numbers. In the villages of India, the schools of Japan, and the cities of China, millions of lithographed books are in use today.

In the time since Senefelder proudly pulled his first copy from the damp stone, lithography has made an enduring mark on history. The materials, the methods, and the machinery are different. But the basic principles established by its inventor have remained unchanged.

Aloys Senefelder's story might be summed up in a series of contrasts—black ink and white paper, grease and water, frustrating problems and final triumph.

Senefelder began with modest goals, seeking only a cheap and simple way to print his plays. Though his plays are long forgotten, his invention thrives. He did not merely improve longstanding methods of printing—he devised an entirely new one.

Lithography has helped men to grope their way toward freedom by means of the printed image and the printed word. Today the story of lithography is reaching its climax—books in great quantity and of high quality are being produced through the newest electronic technology, making possible education on a vast scale. It is fulfilling Aloys Senefelder's dream that his method, which began with the stone, would someday benefit mankind across the earth.

A hundred and fifty years ago he said, "I desire that soon lithography shall spread over the whole world, bringing much good to humanity, and that it may work toward man's progress but never be misused for evil purposes. This grant the Almighty! Then may the hour be blessed in which I invented it!"

Suggestions for Further Reading

Arnold, Edmund C. *Ink on Paper*. New York: Harper & Row, 1963.

This useful handbook on the graphic arts contains an explanation of printing methods and terms.

Foster, Joanna. *Pages, Pictures, and Print: A Book in the Making*. New York: Harcourt, Brace & World, 1958.

An absorbing account of how a book is produced, from the manuscript to the final published volume. It includes a section on printing books by offset lithography.

Heller, Jules. *Printmaking Today*. New York: Holt, Rinehart & Winston, 1958.

This manual shows the entire process of making a lithograph from stone: graining and preparing the surface, drawing the image, working in color, pulling the prints. Other print-making processes are also explained.

Rogers, Frances. *Painted Rock to Printed Page*. Philadelphia: J. B. Lippincott Co., 1960.

Against the background of the earliest forms of communication, the story of printing is brought up to Benjamin Franklin's print shop in the American colonies, and finally to modern times.

Simon, Irving B. *The Story of Printing*. Irvington-on-Hudson: Harvey House, 1964.

In simple language, the author describes all the major printing processes. There is a chapter on "Offset Lithography–A Growing Giant," a glossary of printing terms, and a section for the young editor on how to work with the printer.

Zigrosser, Carl. *The Book of Fine Prints*. New York: Crown, 1965.

The story of fine print-making, from Chinese stone-rubbing to modern techniques, is told by an expert. The book covers etchings, woodcuts, and engravings, as well as lithographs.

Index

S. CARL HIRSCH's first science book for young people, *The Globe for the Space Age,* won the Thomas Alva Edison Foundation Award for the Best Science Book for Children published in 1963. In addition, Mr. Hirsch has written *This is Automation, Fourscore . . . and More: The Life Span of Man,* and *The Living Community: A Venture into Ecology.*

Mr. Hirsch was born in Chicago, and he and his wife now reside in Evanston, Illinois. He is a map lithographer, which accounts for his interest in the history of lithography.